TALES OF RAMAYANA :
WISDOM THROUGH AGES

T. Krishna Dinesh

Tales of Ramayana : Wisdom through Ages
T. Krishna Dinesh

Published by Qurate Books Pvt. Ltd.

© T. Krishna Dinesh

Published in 2023

ISBN: 978-93-5898-709-6

Qurate Books Pvt. Ltd.
Goa 403523, India
www.quratebooks.com
Tel: 1800-210-6527, Email: info@quratebooks.com

Preface

This is taken from Ramayana is an all-popular epic in South and Southeast Asia. It is the one of the two "Itihasa" most widely read & widely revered by hindus. "Itihasa" means happened and true story. It is the story of King Rama who must save his kidnapped wife, Sita.

Along the way, it teaches Hindu life lessons. The Ramayana is told and retold orally, through literature, plays, movies and is reference in many other forms of popular culture today.

Dedication

I would like to thank everyone.
Who are sincerely book lovers?
My family and friends.
Finally to my caring, supporting and loving parents my deepest gratitude.
Your encouragement when the time is tough is much appreciated and duly noticed.
My Heartfelt thanks.

Acknowledge

"I would like to take this opportunity to thank my publishing team."

"Thanks to everyone on the Book in the team who helped me so much".

I cannot express enough thanks to my book team for their continued support.

I offer my sincere appreciation for the learning and opportunity

To The book lovers,

I hope this book helps you to get you out of your work and take you to the world of love.

I would love nothing more than seeing the book in your hands everywhere –Readers walking down the streets, the browser's in a book store, at home.

That's a great challenge which lies ahead of me but it is certainly worth an attempt.

Take out time from your busy schedule to rejoice.

Hope you read and Enjoy.

Disclaimer

This is a work of fiction.

All the characters depicted are imaginary and any resemblance to real person or dead is purely coincidental.

The content of the book reflects the author expression and opinion solely.

As work of fiction & imagination it doesn't not claim scriptural authenticity

Chapter 1

Introduction

Birth of Deva and Rakshasa

Before creating the life Lord Sri Maha Vishnu is in Yoga Nidra(Spiritual sleep) and from Lord Sri Maha Vishnu Lord Brahma was born from Nabhi.(Naval) Lord Brahma was Creator of the life. He first created water, life was crested from that water form. Some Life forms said we will protect this water and some water said they will pray this water. The one who said we will protect the water became the "Rakshasa" and One who said we will pray became "Deva or Yakshulu".

Some people in the "Rakshasa" instead of protecting they started destroying it due to that the "Rakshasa" got bad name. Among the "Rakshasa" who was created by the Lord Brahma the most powerful once are "Hati" & "Prahati". Among them "Prahati" was good who mind his own work and dint bother others. "Hati" was always Hungry for Something.

MahiRavana is the son of the sage Vishrava & brother of Ravana and in some verses he is friend of Ravana. He is the king of the Patal. In some versions of the Ramayana such as the Krittivasi Ramanyana. AhiRavana is also called MahiRavana. He is also called as Maiyarap.

He was one of the son of Ravana and king of Patal and sorcerer, ardent devotee of Goddess Kali & Mahamaya & Chandi. Mahiravana is seen only in Rama- Ravana Yuddha only. After the death of Indrajit's Ravana summons his other son MahiRavaana .

Vibhashana finds out it and inform this to Sri Rama about Mahi Ravana. God Hanuman who is the Devotee of Bhagavan Sri Rama makes a pledge to stand guard to the Rama, Lakshmana where the two brothers are resting.

Hanuman made his tail like a fortress and stood as the guard sitting at the height of so tall that he can see anything & everything protecting the Rama & Lakshmana and also Vanara army in it. Then Bhagavan of Lanka Ravana meet the MahiRavana and speaks like this your I came here indeed of your help you're the ruler of Patal loka, greater sorcerer ever Hanuman has built a fort using his tail and protecting the Ram & Lakshmana along with Vanara sena.

If this one night surpass Bhagavan Ram will definitely kill me that's why in any case you deceive the Hanuman and bring the Ram & Lakshmana to the patal loka. Ravana Asura speak like this on hearing the help from the great Lankaeswara MahiRavana feel Happy and says like this O, Ravana I will do anything which you seek and do it he says and send Ravana to his Palace.

After Ravana left the palace MahiRavana send Suchimuki (one who face is shaped like sharp needle) Rakshasa and told him you're the man of great ideas you dig the earth & make a way inside the fortress of the Hanuman, bring the Rama & Lakshmana.

Then suchimuki starts digging the land in that area but Hanuman Tail Fortress hits him and his face was broken he will die on the spot in that way he was failed to do the task which was assigned to him. Then MahiRavana will send another Rakshasa called Muchikamuni on seeing the invincible Tail Fortress of Hanuman he will try to hit the Tail of Hanuman his head will also broke like that of Suchimuki.

Then MahiRavana will send the PachanaBadi. Hanuman will break his teeth and face in the same way as the Suchimuki's & Muchikamuni and he will flee to the Patal Loka.

Then MahiRavana will turn into Vibhishan and go to the place where Ram& Lakshmana were present.He speaks like this to the Hanuman O Mahaveera, in the night time the Rakshasa have been roaming in this lands and you should be very cautious. I will go inside & see how the Rama, Lakshmana are there. I need your permission to go inside, then Hanuman see Vibhishan as friend then MahiRavana goes inside in between Hanuman legs and goes inside he uses the Portion (Avushedam) on them then shrink them into small size and keep them in a box and keep a piece of his royal cloth and cover it.

Then he came outside and says to everyone that they are safe inside and says you should protect everyone like this. Within few seconds he reaches his Patal Loka. After MahiRavana leaves the fortress Ravana brothers Vibhishan comes to Hanuman, Rakshasa will rome in Mayava form in front of us inform of eagle and donkeys are roaming like that.

If this night surpass Rama Lakshmana will be grateful and win the war O Mahaveera, Sugriva palieta Vanara army is in your control and in bravery, strength, well knowledge there is no one like you and you are everything for us don't let anyone pass into this Fortress. I want to see the Rama, Lakshmana after hearing this Hanuman get suspicious and say like this just now only you have seen them. why did come again tell me what you're thinking say clearly he asks the Vibhishan .

My uncle MahiRavana is great sorcerer, he must have taken my form let us go inside and take a look at Prabhu Ram, Lakshmana then on going inside the Ram, Lakshmana are not there inside. Then Hanuman Realize what has happened went quickly to Rescue the Ram & Lakshmana.

He takes Ram & Lakshmana to Patal Loka through present-day Horton's Plains in Sri Lanka. Since Mahiravana is an ardent worshipper of Goddess Kali, he starts making preparations to offer the 2 brothers as a sacrifice to please Her.

Hanuman ask the Vibhishan what is the way to Patal loka after knowing way hanuman reaches there like wind's speed reached the gates of Patal loka. He was stopped by Makaradhwaja, who tells him that he is His son. God Hanuman is surprised, as He is a brahmachari (a celibate bachelor). Then Hanuman ask the story the Makardhwaja says like this when you are crossing Lanka from your sweat a small drop has been fallen into a river and a Alligator has swallowed it and from it stomach I was born and became Makardhwaja.

After knowing the story of Makaradhwaja, He asks him to let Him inside. Makaradhwaja says it is his Dharma (righteous duty) to protect the gates of Patala-loka. He cannot fail in performing his duty even if it means fighting his father. There is a fierce fight and Makaradhwaja is defeated.

God Hanuman then transforms Himself into a bee and enters Patala-loka. He approaches Goddess Kali and asks Her for help. Even though Mahiravana is an ardent devotee, he is clearly on the wrong path. The goddess explains a plan to God Hanuman, which He whispers to God Rama and Lakshmana.

Mahiravana summons the 2 brothers, asking God Rama to put His head on the sacrificial altar. God Rama says He has never bowed before anyone in His life and asks Mahiravana to demonstrate how. When the foolish Mahiravana bends his head on the altar, God Hanuman transforms from a bee into His real self but with 5 faces. He simultaneously blows out the 5 lamps in the room, grabs Mahiravana's sword and beheads him. Thus, devotees worship God Hanuman as a pancha-mukhi (a 5-faced) deity.

God Hanuman then also kills Mahiravana's son Ahiravana.

Source: **Krittivasa Ramayana 6.446-496; 'Essence of the Fifth Veda' by Gaurang Damani pages 49-50.**

Other version:

Airavana and Mairavan were friends of Ravana. These rule the netherworld. Ravana sends for his messengers to get their help in defeating Rama and Lakshmana in the battle.

In the battle, Bhagavan Rama defeats Ravana, destroys his chariot, crown. He gives Ravana a second chance. After thinking Ravana sends for the help of these two rakshasas who were experts in occult. They worship Kamakshi devi in Patala. They have shape shifting powers. After taking orders from Ravana, they go to Vanara's camp in search of the Ikshvaku brothers Rama and Lakshmana resting on a rock. The rakshasas kidnap them tied to those rocks. The rakshasas take Rama and Lakshmana into a cave in the Patala.

Hanuman finds that Rama and Lakshmana were missing in the camp and goes searching them. He hears two pigeons talking that they found two Rakshasas taking up two strong men into netherworld. Hanuman goes to patala and searches there. There he finds a vanara who is none other than Makaradhwaja, son of Hanuman. A conversation takes place between them which I gave in an answer of mine. He blesses him and goes out searching for the Ikshvaku princes. He finds a large goddess's idol in a temple near the cave.

He then enters the temple in an atomic size and talks in the voice of goddess addressing Airavan and Mairavan who have been worshipping her for a long time. Hanuman asks them to bring delicious food items for her (the goddess) and also good clothes and weapons for Bhagavan Rama and Lakshmana. He orders them to bring them alive and not dead. They feel happy that the goddess is happy with their worship and does the same.

After sometime, Rama and Lakshmana wake up. They take up the weapons and fight the rakshasas. Rama kills them both but they revive again. It happens again but they are not dead. Hanuman thinks that there is some death secret involved in killing these rakshasa duo. He wanders here and there in search of a way to kill them. Then he finds a woman sitting alone in a garden. She is wife of Airavan (bhoga patni).

He asks details of her and she replies she is a Naga kanya who was enjoyed forcibly by Airavan. She says they both ill treated her and given grief. She agrees to give out the secret of Airavana and Mairavana's death on one condition.

The condition is when she becomes Bhagavan Rama's wife. Hanuman agrees and goes back to the place where Rama and Lakshmana were fighting. Long time ago, Airavana and Mairavana saved a huge colony of honey bees from children. As a gratitude, they were protecting Airavan and Mairavan. They collect valuable elixir (amrit) and purify the blood of the duo. Hence, they can't be killed when the colonies of honey bees are alive. She says there are crores of bees in the palace of Airavan and Mairavan. After hearing this, Hanuman goes to their palace immediately and kills them except a single bee which sought refugee of Hanuman. Hanuman sends this bee to Nagakanya's gynaeceum and eats out the legs of bed she is resting and stay silent. The rest of the work of killing Rakshasas was done by Rama. He kills both the Rakshasas. Here ends the story of Airavana and Mairavana.

Now, Hanuman requests Rama and Lakshmana to visit Naga kanya's palace as she has helped them killing two rakshasas. Rama agrees to that request. They saw different artifacts, pictures present in the palace. She asks Rama to sit as a mark of receiving guests. When Bhagavan Rama sits on the bed smiling at her, the bed which was already majorly damaged by bee fell down due to his weight. This was counted as Naga Kanya being wife of Rama without Rama not actually marrying or doing anything. She was satisfied with it. She then gets ready to jump into fire. Bhagavan Rama gives a boon to her that she will be reborn as a Brahmin lady in the Dwapara Yuga and he will marry her. She was born as Kanyakumari whom Bhagavan Krishna marries.

Reference: **Ananda Ramayana Sara Kanda, Sarga 11.**

Chapter 2

Ravaṇa sends help-cry for Ahiravaṇa and Mahiravana

Following Kumbhkarana's demise, Ravana sends for the two brothers - Ahiravana and Mahiravana, who lives in a city called - Mahikavati, in Patala - requesting them to arrange a kidnap-murder of Sri Rama & Laksmana.

After hearing Ravana's plight from the messenger, both Ahiravana and Mahiravana, after propitiating goddess Ambika for good-luck, deliberate on ways to vanquish the Daśarath's sons (Rama & Laksmana).

Hanumana meets his son, Makardhvaja

Both the demon brothers reach the war arena at Lanka, to capture Rama & Laksmana, but find no luck on account of Hanuman's impenetrable security-patrol using his tail. Thus, they further propitiate goddess Kamaksi to gain an advantage.

Thus, Hanuman retracts his patrol, and at midnight the demon brother kidnaps the Daśarath nandanas, and takes them to Patala-loka.

Hanuman somehow realizes Rama & Laksmana are missing, and thus through a spur of 'divine-inspiration', he propitiates goddess Adi-Sakti and realizes the whereabouts of his Bhagavan .

Hanuman reaches the demon city under the disguise of a sage and meets (and fights with) his son - Makardhvaja. When realization dawns upon both father and son of each other's real identity, they call off the fight.

Mahiravana's death

Hanuman sings the glory of his Bhagavan to his son, and when he finds his son in the dharma dilemma (to betray his demon over Bhagavan at the expense of helping his father?), Hanuman becomes invisible and leaves to find his Bhagavan . As midnight approaches, he finally finds Sri Rama being brought to the sacrificial-altar to be sacrificed by rakshasas under the guidance of Mahiravana.

At the penultimate moment of sacrifice, Sri Rama remembers Hanuman a, and thus, Hanuman removes his invisibility illusion and finally kills Mahiravana, along with hordes of demons.

Ahiravana's death

As Mahiravana is killed at the hands of Hanuman a, a big fight ensues and Sri Rama, Lakshmana, and Hanuman obliterate the demonic forces swiftly.

Watching his forces deplete, Ahiravana approaches the arena. Ahiravana had a boon from god Siva similar to the demon called - Raktabija, thus on being hit and wounded by Sri Rama's arrows, as drops of Ahiravana's blood trickle down, multiple clones of Ahiravana manifests on the war arena.

Finding his Bhagavan in an impasse to kill the demon-Bhagavan, Hanuman reaches for Ahiravana's wife (who became enamoured of Sri Rama) for help, and on being assured a marriage proposal from Hanuman to marry Rama, she agrees to divulge Ahiravana's boon secrets.

Ahiravana's wife - Chandrasena, explains how her husband propitiated Siva through an extreme penance by piercing his toe with a lance, and on this account, Siva, happy with his penance, awarded him a boon similar to demon Raktabija.

And thus, whenever a drop of Ahiravana's blood falls on the ground, the bees lingering on the forehead of Siva transports the amrita drops (from a pot kept in Patala-loka itself) and impregnates the demons' fallen blood drops with life, and thus a new Ahiravana manifests immediately.

And hearing this, immediately, Hanuman rushes for the amrita-pot to demolish it.

As Hanuman obliterates the pot along with the bees, an Akasa-vani informs Sri Rama that now Ahiravana is vulnerable, and thus, without wasting a single second, Sri Rama mounts the 'Agni-Banain his arrow and charges it at Ahiravana with sacred mantras, and thus, the demon dies, as every drop of blood gets evaporated instantly from the ensuing fire.

Rama citing his 'eka-Patni-Vrata as the reason to not marry Chandrasena, promises her marriage, in his next appearance on Earth as Sri Krishna, and, Chandrasena thus, shall be born as Satyabhāmā (daughter of king Satrajit). And finally, Sri Rama and Lakshmana leaves for Lanka on the shoulders of Hanuman a.

Source : **The Bhavartha Ramayana**

Chapter 3

Some of unknown characters in Ramayana

Ruma:
Wife of Sugriva and younger sister of Tara. Ramayana mentions about the qualities of Tara, her wisdom and devotion towards her husbands which makes one among Panchkanya. But Ramayana neglects Ruma, whom in my opinion is as good as Tara.

Ruma and Sugriva fell in love with each other. But ruma's Father disagrees to this, as he wanted both of his daughters to be the wife of Vaali, who is the king of Khiskinda.

He wanted both of his daughters to be queens. But Sugriva & Ruma elopes with the help of Hanuman.

Vaali was Ruma's brother in law in two ways, as he was the elder brother of her husband and also her elder sister's husband. But Vaali clouded by anger due to misunderstandings between Sugriva, forcefully stops Ruma who was going to accompany her husband.

This women loved Sugriva so much that she eloped from her parental home, her husband without a second thought runs for his life leaving his wife to suffer vaali's anger.

Vaali forced himself on her though he stood her father's position by relationship. Her sister Tara couldn't do anything to help her so as her parents. Her son was too small to fight for her. Ruma was a big devotee to Bhagavan Vishnu.

She believed Bhagavan will save her from all miseries and get justice to her. True to her belief Bhagavan himself came, killed Vaali for lusting a women who stood in his daughters position. Once when her husband was back he had to take her sister as his wife as per the rule. Ruma never complained for making Tara the chief queen and Angad as crown prince. Neither had she blamed her husband for running away leaving her under Vaali. In my opinion ruma's story teaches us many things. But yet she was ignored despite of giving much morals to us.

Sulochana:

She was the wife of Indrajeet or Meghanad son of Ravan. She was also the daughter of Adisesha & Nagalakshmi (who reincarnated as Lakshmana & Urmila).

Meghnad who has got all powerful astras from brahma and also a boon that he will be killed only by a man who has not slept, ate or had physical relationship (which was humanly impossible) sets to conquer world. He wins Devaloka by defeating Indra and then he sets to conquer Nagalok, defeats Vasuki - king of serpents.

Vasuki curses Meghnada that he will be killed by his elder brother Sheshnag (who was the strongest snake). To undo the curse Meghnad kidnaps seshnag's daughter Sulochana and marries her, thinking that Sheshnag will not kill his son in law.

But Lakshmana who was the reincarnation of Sheshnag kills him. Sulochana being a devotee of Vishnu was prohibited to pray him in Lañkā by her husband but she never complained. She was a brave woman who sent her husband to the battle field without tears. Post her husband's death she meets Lakshmana and makes it clear to him that it was not Lakshmana's victory but Urmila's love and sacrifice that had made Meghnad's death possible.

So it was Urmila who had won not Lakshmana. She went on sati leaving her kid to Mondadori.

Sarama:

She was a Gandharva princess and wife of Vibhushan. Just like her husband she too was an adherent devotee of Bhagavan Vishnu & followed the path of dharma.

She was with Sita in ashokavatika when Sita was in Lañkā. She became a true friend of Sita and informed all the details of war to Sita.

Trijata:

Daughter of Vibhushan and sarama. She too served Sita in ashokavatika along with her mother.

She was also a devotee of Rama. Post war, she prays to Rama that in next birth she wanted belong in his family.

Because of which she was reborn as Subhadra. (few book says Subhadra was a form of Parvathi or yoga Maya.)

Shanta:

Bhagavan rama's elder sister. She was Dasharatha daughter in Kausalya who was given in hand of adoption to Kausalya's cousin brother Anga desa chakravathi who name is Rom path and Rani Varshani.

Because they have no children so he gave her to them. They look after her with love and care. Later she got married to rishishringa .

One day when she is roaming the palace with her father Rom path then a poor Brahmin will come there he ask help for the but on that day she ignores the Brahmin.

That Brahmin is the worshiper of Bhagavan indra, seeing his devotee in that indra get angry on Rom Path and didnt have a rain on that kingdom.

She after knowing that her adopted kingdom is suffer from drought due to a curse, which can be done only if a sage who has not known women will do Yagna.

Rom Path ask for help rishishringa according to his advice he performances a Yagna.

Then in the kingdom rains will starts. Then Rom Path marries his daughter to rishishringa. He performed yagna and saves the kingdom from drought and also he performs yagna for Dasharatha because of which Bhagavan ram and his brothers were born.

In my opinion she was less spoken despite of playing a pivotal role.

Shrutakirti:

Younger cousin sister of Sita and wife of ram's brother Shatrughan. We all know the story of Urmila & Mandhavi because of the sacrifices made by them.

But shrutakirti despite of being equally good as her sisters is less spoken. It was she along with Bharatha who stopped Shatrughana from killing Mandara for being the root cause of ram's exile.

When Rama was crowned as the king post his exile, he asked all his family members to ask for something.

Everyone asked his blessings but shrutakirti asked for his robes which he wore during exile. This demand surprised Rama.

When he questioned why she need his exile robes she answered that normally sons accept kingship from fathers at their young age but Rama accepted exile in his youth which was a path breaking decision. So even his exile robes needed to be worshipped just like ram. Dasharatha actually had 4 gems in the form of daughter in laws.

Dhanyamalini

Second wife of Ravan and younger sister of vidhyjiva who was shoorpanaka's husband. She bored 3 sons to Ravana who all were killed in war. Of which Atikāya is popular.

Maya:

Elder sister of mandhodhari and daughter of Mayasura. She was married to king Shambhar. Ravana while conquering world reaches shambar's kingdom.

But he lusts for beautiful Maya forgetting that she is his sister in law. He traps her in his magic. Shambhar fights with him and dies.

Post shambar's death Ravan approaches Maya to be his wife but she commits sati by cursing him that his lust for someone else wife will be the cause of his death.

Vajramala:

Wife of Kumbhakarna. Kumbakarna despite of his giant size was soft hearted person. Despite of his curse like boon because of which he sleeps 6 months never complaint about his fate. He loved his wife so much.

She too was a devoted wife who accepts that her husband has to go to sleep for 6 months. Because of kumbhakarna's loyalty towards his brother (he knew his brother was wrong, still he fought for him as it was his duty as a brother) this women not only loses her husband but also her sons too. She was also the sister of Mahabali.

Ilavida:

Mother of Kubera and stepmom of Ravana. Her husband vishravas left her for his second wife Kaikasi - an Asuras princess. When Ravan conquers Lañkā vishravas goes back to his first wife leaving his second family.

Tataka:

Grandmother of Ravana. Mother of Kaikasi, Subaru and mariachi. Her husband Somali was the real owner of Lañkā (which was created by Vishwakarma).

Bhagavan Vishnu captures Lañkā in a war and crows Kubera as the king of Lañkā. She along with her husband encourages her younger daughter Kaikasi to marry vishravas who was father of Kubera.

She was extremely beautiful and has mastered in the art of magic. She was the one who taught magic to her granddaughter Shurpanakha or Minakshi. She was cursed by sage Agastya for ruining his yagna to lose her beauty and become a monster. She was killed by Rama.

Kumbini:

Cousin sister of Ravan. Her husband dies while fighting for Ravan in war. Her son lavanasura was killed by Shatrughan during Rama's crow nation ceremony.

Post her son's death she stayed back in Lañkā along with Vibhushan.

Aruni:

She was the female form of Aruna who was the charioteer of surya and elder brother of Garuda.

Once he learns about a magical kingdom in heaven created by Vishwakarma were only women were allowed to enter. A curious Aruna transforms into a female called Aruni and visits the place. She was seen by Indra and he gets attracted to her.

She consents his desire and sleeps with Indra and give birth to Vaali. When surya hears about aruni's story he request Aruna to take aruni's form. Surya gets attracted to her and the consummate, sugreeva was born as a result of their union.

Indumathi:

Wife of King Aja & mother of Dasharatha. She was a beautiful and delicate princess. Post the birth of Dasharatha, once she was roaming in royal garden, narada's garland from sky falls on her head and she dies immediately.

Actually a Indumati was a cursed apsara named Harini, who was cursed to be born as a human. Her curse will be liberated once narada's garland fells on her head.

Suvarchala:

Suvarchala an apsara was very impulsive and often acted without thinking. Once because of her impulsive behaviour, Bhagavan Brahma got very angry with her and cursed her that she would become a bird.

Suvarchala promised Bhagavan Brahma that she had repented her ways. Bhagavan Brahma said that his words could not be taken back and that Suvarchala would have to go to earth and stay as a bird. Bhagavan Brahma however modified the curse and said that Suvarchala was to be freed from her curse if she touched the pudding given by Bhagavan Agni to Dasaratha.

Kartiveeryarjun:

He was a King with ten hands. He has defeated Ravan in a dual match.

Sampati:

The elder brother of Jatayu & son of Aruna- the charioteer of surya in his wife Sheilya. Once in childhood sampati & Jatayu has a flying competition.

Jatayu flies so high that he reaches sun. To protect Jatayu from sunrays, sampati covers him with his wings. Thus due to sunburn sampati loses his both wings forever.

Lavanasura:

Son of Kumbini. He created havoc in the earth post the death of his Ravan. Shatrughna bravely fights with him & kills him.

Kesari:

The father of Hanuman. He was the Senapati of Kishkinda. He once saved Añjanā from a demon & eventually she gets married to him.

Kesari along with Añjanā undergoes severe penance for obtaining a son like shiva. Thus Shivaansh Hanuman is born to them.

Nal & Neel:

They are vanaras in the group of sugreeva. Nal was the son of Vishwakarma. Neel was the son of Agni.

Nal has a great knowledge of architecture from his father, whereas Neel was blessed that anything he throws into ocean will not dive. Thus Nal and Neel creates Sethubandhanam, the bridge to cross lanka.

Goddess suvarchala :

She is the daughter of Bhagavan surya narayana and the wife of Bhagavan Hanuman.

Sahastravan :

Perhaps the Strongest demon in all of the versions of Ramayana combined, He Defeated all the Gods and conquered heavens as well and was a million times powerful than Dashanan Ravana.

He and His army were Slaughtered By Maa sita, When she assumed the fierce Form of Mahakali.

Neela :

He was the son of Demon king vibhisan, and The greatest devotee of Bhagavan Hanuman.

Laksashira :

His mention can be Found In the Vilanka Ramayan, and was almost as powerful as Sahastravana.

Due to his Power, everyone including Indra, kubera, vishwakarma, Demons, Gandharvas, celestials and Other Gods were scared of Him. He managed to overpower Sri Ram, Lakshmanaji and Hanumanji in a battle (and was also defeated twice by Hanumanji).

He was finally killed by Mata sita, Who assumed the Form of mahakali to complete the task, within a single strike of Sword.

Kalnemi :

A powerful, shape shifting demon, who was sent by Ravana, to stop Bhagavan Hanuman from fetching herbs for Lakshmana ji, but was Killed by him Instead.

Mulkasura :

The son of Kumbhakarna, who was abandoned by his father when he was born. He was an extremely powerful demon, and was killed by Goddess chandika form of chaya sita (an ansha of mata sita).

Tarasena :

As per Kritivasi Ramayana, he was the son of Vibhisanji, And was also a great devotee of Sri Ram. when He arrived in the warzone, He was covered with the name of Sri Ram on his entire body, and Rath as well, which made him almost invincible. He was later killed by Sri Ram only.

Kewat :

A boatman who was a great devotee of Bhagavan Rama, He helped The Trio to cross river ganga, during their exile.

Kagbhusandi :

One of the Greatest devotees of Bhagavan Ram, who narrated Ramayana, much before Sage Valmiki or Goswami tulsidasji. He is said to have seen ramayanas of multiple kalpas.

Chapter 4

Some versions of Ramayana where it meet happy ending?

In Padmapurana'a patal khand, it was written that sita had come again ayodhya with luv and kusha and lived 11000 years long with Bhagavan Rama. After that Rama & family with all ayodhya's resident taken "samadhi" in sarayu river.

Luv set city of Lahoure (now in pakistan) and kusha stayed in ayodhya and ruled the city. Not much said about him because after some year of rama's nirvan there is change of yuga (dwapar arrived).

Bharat's son pushkal set peshawar city (now in pakistan) and shatrughans' son set mathura city & lakshaman's son set lakhnow on in UP.

How did Ramayana end? What Happened to Rama after sita incarnated?

One day Yama Dharma Raja came to intimate Rama that his time is over and he needed to return to Vaikunta. Since these were Deva rahasya, Yama insisted Rama that they should be alone while discussing this. Rama made

Lakshmana guard the room where both Rama and Yama was discussing.

Meanwhile, Dhurvasa Maharishi came to the palace and asked Lakshmana to let him inside to meet Rama. Lakshmana first hesitated but due to the temperamental character of Dhurvasa, who was famous for cursing anybody anywhere without a thought, Lakshmana sent him in. Once Dhurvasa went in, Rama did all the ceremonies which were apt for a Maharishi.

Dhurvasa, very pleased, blessed Rama and left. Yama also left the place. However, Rama was furious with Lakshmana for breaking the vow. Lakshmana became very sad as he had not been away from Rama for lifetime and so he went to Forest and left his mortal body and reached Vaikunta as Adhisesha.

Rama who already missed Sita who was taken by her mother Bhooma Devi, missed Lakshmana too. Bhratha and Shatrukna were also missing.

Rama then understood what Yama had told him and he went to Sarayu Nadhi. Where along with people of Ayodya, he jumped into the river and left his mortal body and reached Vaikunta, where Sita - Lakshmi, Lakshmana - Adhisesha, Bharatha and Shatrukna - The Sanga and Chakra were waiting for Rama - Mahavishnu. This is the end of Ramayana

Why did Rama divide the kingdom between Kush and Luv?

Bhagavan Rama had two sons therefore he had to equally bestow and divide his kingdom Ayodhya.

Padma Purana states about sons of Bhagavan Rama.

"Kusha and Lava were sons of Bhagavan Rama; those of Lakshman were Angad and Chandraketu; sons of Bharata were Taksha and Pushkar; and Subáhu and Śúrasen were Śatrughna's sons."

Ayodhya was then abandoned after Bhagavan Rama went into Sarayu river with Bharata and Shatrughna and their wives.

Bhagavan Rama made made his son Lava ruler of Shravasti which was North Kosala . He also founded city of Lava puri. Kusha founded Kushavati(Kusasthali) place which became capital of Kosala kingdom. It is said Kusha ruled Kashmir, Indus River and Hindu Kush as frontier lands of India known as Hindu Kush Kshetra.

Bhagavan Lakshman's sons who were Angad and Chandraketu ruled countries near Himalayas whose capital (s) were Angadi and Chandravaktra. Bharata's sons Taksha and Pushkar were sovereigns of Gandharapradesh but they both lived within Takshashila and Pushkaravati. Śatrughna's sons Subahu and Surasen ruled Mathura.

Bhagavan Rama had four siblings therefore kingdom had to be divided. Bhagavan Rama was eldest son of Dashratha. Therefore Lava and Kusha inherited their father's kingdom Kosala. Shatrughna slayed Lavana who was son of demon Madhu and became ruler of Mathura therefore his sons inherited Mathura. Bhagavan Lakshman's sons also ruled countries within Himalayas and maybe we may say these two sons founded these places or inherited these from their father.

Where are the future generation after Luv and Kush?

Rama Bhupala's sons were Kusa And Lava. Kusa was eligible for main powers as king according to the rules of Ishwaka, as he was elder one. Sons of Lakshmana were Angada and Chithraketha. Thaksha and Pushkara were sons of Bharatha.

Subahu and Surasena were born to Sathrughna. Kusa's wife was belonged to Chandra Vamsa. Now I will give Ancestral tree of Kusa.

King Kusa — —- Athidhi — — Nishadha — — Nala Nabhasa — — — Pundareeka — — Kshemadhanva — —- Devaanika — —- Ahinaaga — —- Paaripathra — — — Dala — — Chhala — — Ukthha — — Vajranaabha — —- Sankhanabha — — —- Hiranyanabha.

Hiranya Nabha sacrificed his kings life for the purpose of great knowledge belonging to Parabrahma. He learned Vedantha near Jaimini (disciple of Vyasa Bhagavan), and taught Yogavidya to Yaagnavalkya.

Hiranyanabha — — Pushya — — — Dhruvasandhi — — — Sudarsana — — Agni varna — — Seeghra — —- Maraa

Mara is Chiranjeevi. I.e., he has no death. He has now no attachments, having self-control. He is now in Kalaapa village. He will be main person (Maha Purusha) of Surya (Sun) dynasty's kings in future Yuga.

Mara — —- Prasusrutha — —- Susandhi — — Amarsha — — Mahaśwantha — —- Viśruthavantha — — Bruhadbala.

Abhimanyu killed Bruhadbala on 13th day of Maha Bharatha Sangram, who fought against Pandavas supporting Kauravas. Mangalam. Subham bhuyaat

Chapter 5

Some events which happened after Ramayana?

Rama slayed the king Brahma Putra Ravan on the tenth day of the battle by striking his arrow at Ravana,s Navel, which is where the nectar of immortality was stored.

Rama direct Lakshmana to crown Vibhishana as the king of Lanka on Rams advice and Sita is then brought to Rama,s Presence.

Vibhishana arranges for an aerial car called Pushpaka Vimana to transport Rama and others to Ayodhya. In the course of flight Rama shows the whole city of and other places to sita.

Pushpaka Vimana lands at Nandigrama,outskirts of Ayodhya. Bharata welcomes everyone. Rama and sita are coronated as king and queen of Ayodhya respectively in glorious celebration.

Doubts again arise over sita purity as Rama over hears people of the kingdom speaking of ill about them. People say that Rama shouldn't have accepted sita as she lived in Ravana Abode.

Rama abandons pregnant sita, instructs Lakshmana take her to forest and leave her there. Dejected, Devastated, sita stays in sage Valmiki Ashram and adopts a new name called "Vanadevi".

There sita gives birth to twin sons, Lava and Kusa. They were educated and trained in sakala kala under the sage Valmiki.

They also learned the story Rama how great he was. However Lava and Kusa were not not told that Rama was their father and vanadevi , their mother was sita.

Chapter 6

Some stories in Ramayana

The Squirrel's Tale:

Following Sita's kidnapping, Bhagavan Rama and his army of monkeys and bears begin construction on a bridge spanning the ocean to connect them to Lanka. The enthusiasm, commitment, and degree of energy displayed by Bhagavan Rama's soldiers throughout the bridge's building brought him great joy. A young squirrel was putting a pebble she had in her mouth next to the boulders.

She did it effortlessly and repeatedly. A monkey suddenly spotted her and began making fun of her. He warned her not to approach should a boulder topple her. Everyone started making fun of her when they heard this. This squirrel was sobbing.

From a distance, Bhagavan Rama was observing all of this. The squirrel was upset and went to Bhagavan Rama to complain about everyone. The Army was then shown by Bhagavan Rama how the squirrel's stone served as a link between the two boulders. Even she adds value that rivals that of the other soldiers.

Bhagavan Rama rubbed the squirrel's back in appreciation for his effort. His fingerprints from the strokes are visible on the squirrel's body. The squirrels have worn white stripes on their bodies ever since.

Hanuman's refused to Bhagavan Rama's command

After the coronation ceremony, Bhagavan Hanuman was depressed. He closed his eyes though he sat in a corner and meditated on Bhagavan Rama. His eyes were continuously flowing tears.

When Sita became aware of this, she promptly alerted Bhagavan Rama. Rama responded as he turned to face Hanuman, "I am unable to offer you anything in exchange for your devotion and bhakti.

The only option I have is to take you to Vaikuntai ". Hanuman asked, "Bhagavan Mahavishnu is the cause, and Bhagavan Rama is the effect. As asked, "Will you be with me in Vaikunta?," Bhagavan Rama answered, "Yes, but not as Rama, but as Bhagavan Mahavishnu." Hanuman replied, "When Bhagavan Rama wasn't there, I would never go there. I will stay in Ayodhyai and continue meditating on Bhagavan Rama".

Rama's sister Shanta's Narrative

Shanta was the name of King Dashrath's daughter, who was born before Bhagavan Rama. Vershini, the older sister of Kaushalya, never had children. Vershini once made a flippant request for her child when visiting her sister. When Dashratha learned this, he approved her adoption of Shanta, his daughter. According to popular belief, Bhagavan Rama and his other brothers were not informed of their sister.

Was Sita Mandodari's daughter?

The Adbhuta Ramayana claims that Mandodari was Sita's mother, which may come as a shock to most of you. Ravana would preserve the sages' blood in a big pot after he had killed them. Sage Gritsamada was a dedicated devotee of Lakshmi.

In order to get Goddess Lakshmi as his daughter, he even engaged in penance. He collected the milk from the Darbha grass and put it in a pot, purifying it with chants in the hope that Lakshmi would live there. But, Ravana entered Gritsamada's home covertly and added the milk to his pot.

Mandodari made the decision to take her own life by swallowing the blood that Ravana had kept in the pot since she was so angry at his cruel crimes. Because of the milk, Mandodari does not perish but instead becomes pregnant with Sita, one of Lakshmi's incarnations.

Janaka discovers the infant after she abandons it in Kurukshetra.

When Ram order to execute Hanuman

Once Bhagavan Rama succeeded his father as king, Narada could not abide the peace that reigned in the realm. He therefore made an effort to set Ram and Hanuman apart. Hanuman was misled by Narada to greet all the sages except Vishwamitrai when they entered the court because he wasn't a sage by birth. Hanuman followed the advice, which at first did not trouble Vishwamitra.

But after being provoked by Narada, Vishwamitra became furious and demanded with Bhagavan Rama to execute Hanuman.

As a Vishwamitra follower, Rama was unable to disobey his master and hence ordered the shooting of Hanuman.

The next day saw the release of the statement of execution as well. The arrows couldn't harm Hanuman, though.

The Brahmastra, Bhagavan Rama's most powerful weapon, then was used.But before Hanuman, even Brahmastra failed. Do you understand what actually occurred? because of Hanuman's continuous chanting of Bhagavan Rama's name. Narada requested Vishwamitra to resolve the dispute after realising his mistake.

Do you know where the name Bajrangbali came from?

When Sita was applying vermilion to her forehead one day, Hanuman inquired, "Why do you apply vermilion?" "For Bhagavan Rama's longer and healthier life," Sita replied. Hanuman, overjoyed, smeared vermilion all over his body. Bhagavan Rama burst out laughing when he saw Hanuman smeared in Vermilion.

He named him 'Bajrangbali,' which is derived from the word Bajrang, which means 'orange.'

Lakshmana wish to become elder brother to Rama?

Most of us know that Bhagavan Rama is the incarnation of Vishnu, but what about his brothers Lakshmana, Bharat, and Shatrughan?

Bhagavan Rama's Sudarshan-Chakra is Bharat and Shatrughan, and Lakshmana is his Shesh-Naag, Vishnu's seat in Vaikunth.

Later, Lakshmana was born as Balram, Bhagavan Krishna's elder brother. Lakshmana had always complained that because he was born as Ram's younger brother, he had to obey all of Ram's commands. When he was born as Balram, his wish to be an older brother was granted.

Lakshmana Has Been Defying Sleep For 14 Years:

Lakshmana's wife, Urmila, was ready to accompany him when he was ready for journey along with him, but Lakshmana forced her to stay at home. Lakshmana wished to keep Ram and Sita safe from all dangers by defeating sleep. So he approached Nindra, the Goddess of Sleep and asked her to look over him for the next 14 years.

Nindra demanded that someone sleep on his behalf in order to restore balance. So Lakshmana requested that she consider Urmila for this. Nindra went to Ayodhya's palace and asked Urmila if she would like to take over Lakshmana's sleep, which she gladly agreed to.

Urmila slept for 14 years, until Ram's coronation day. Laxman would never have been able to kill Megnath if it hadn't been for Urmila's assistance.

Hanuman has written Ramayana before Valmiki

Hanuman has written Ramayana before Valmiki he has written this with his nails in one stone when Valmiki know about this incident he goes to the stone and observes it. He read the writings of Hanuman was surprised to see how the script was written beautifully he praised hanuman O Pavanputra no can praise and write Ramayana like you. After hearing this from Valmiki he took the stone and threw in it deep sea .

Then onwards Valmiki Ramayana was famous and first work.

In Ramayana the powerful Gayathri Mantra has been mentioned

In Ramayana the powerful Gayathri Mantra has been mentioned in Valmiki Ramayana there are 24000 slokas every 1000 slokas if we take the first letter then we get the

Gayathri mantra with the 24 letters .the Gayathri Mantra has been written.

What is the cause for Seetha swamavaram?

When she is young age she lifted shiva Dhanush very easily then her fathers decided who will lift shiva Dhanush will marry Seetha, medulla Chakravathi Janakudu. That's why Janakudu kept shiva Dhanush at Seetha sawayamvaram Bhagavan Shri Ram will break the bow marrying Seetha Devi.

The name of shiva Dhanush is pinaka.

Did you know Lakshmana had another name?

Lakshmana has another name Godakeshudu. He got this name when he took care of shri ram & Seetha Devi for 14 years vana vasa.

Curse of Tara on shri Ram ?

In the battle shri ram will hide behind a tree strike a arrow at Vali the arrow pierce the Vali he will fall down and this news is heard by his wife Tara then in angry she will curse shri Ram in his next incarnation which is cause for shri Krishna death. Shri Krishna will die when a arrow pierce his toe and dies.

Curse of "Vrinda" on Lord "Vishnu"

According to Hindu scripture, the Tulsi plant was a women named "Vrinda"(Brinda), a synonym of Tulsi. She was married to the demon king "Jalandhar".

Due to her piety and devotion to Vishnu, her husband became invincible. Even God "Shiva", the destroyer in the Hindu Trinity could not defeat "Jalandhar". So, "Shiva" requested "Vishnu" the preserver in the Trinity to find a solution.

"Vishnu" disguised himself as "Jalandhar" and tricked "Vrinda". Her chastity destroyed, "Jalandhar" was killed by "Shiva"."Vrinda" cursed "Vishnu" to become black in colour and he would be separated from his wife.

Thus, he was transformed into black "Shaligram" stone and in his "Ram" avatar, his wife "Sita" was Kidnapped by demon king and thus separated from him.

Chapter 7

Birth of Jambavantha is tied up with Ravana Asura ?

The birth of Jambavantha is linked with the Ravana Asura according to the Utra Ramayana – 10 Sarga refers to Ravana Asura do Tapusu to please Lord Brahma get vara then he ask like this Pakshulu, sarpalu, Yakshalu, Daitulu, Danvalu, Rakshalu, Devathulu, they should never kill me rest of all living beings I don't bother like Manava, Vanara, they are not a threat to me. Brahma agree to these give Varas to the Ravana Asura.

Ravana Asura After getting the Varas from Brahma start to wage wars and start conquering the 14 Loka like Purja, Madjaza, Adho Devatha's went running towards Brahma. They ask Lord Brahma for solution then Brahma takes them to Shri Maha Vishnu, Shri Maha Vishnu speaks like this in my next incarnation which will be in Threata Yuga. I will be born as Manava and kill Ravana Asura he ask Brahma to create Vanara & Baulkhams. In the process of Creation of Vanara & Baulkham s. Jambavantha is born.

There are two versions of Jambavantha birth.

Valmiki Ramayana Balakanda 17 sarga 6 sloka. When Brahma started creating Vanara he was thinking spend much time in it when he yawn as he was sleepy Baulkham was born from it. That is Jambavanthadu he is king of Baulkham's.

Kamba Ramayana -Purva Kanda

World is created by Brahma also has life span 100 years. This 100 years are different then us Krutha Yugam, Threta Yugam, Dwapar Yugam, and Kalie Yugam. When we add all these we get Forty Three Lakhs , Twelve thousands (43,12000)years which is called Maha Yugam. If 1000 Maha Yugam completed then it a day for Brahma if another 1000 completed it's a night for Brahma. Simple 311.04 Trillion years.

Brahma life span is explained in if Kalpam completed then that night Nayamithaka Pralam will come to end in this the world created by Brahma will be drowned by Garbodakam (Cosmic) ocean will be destroyed.

In every Kalpam this will occur then Asura will make havoc. In one Prayalam (when world is about to end) time from Shri Maha Vishnu ears two Rakshasa are born who are Madhu & Kaitabu. Because of Prayalam water level has raised and merged the 14 lokas and came to Brahma Lokam where Brahma was sitting.

The two Rakshasa challenged Brahma for war among the 4 face of Brahma from the middle face a sweat drop has raise and drop from his beard which lead to create Baulkham his name initially is as he was born from Swedam (sweat) jata (beard or hair) Ambujata he first ventured his feet in place Jambunada then people called him Jambavanthaudu.

As Jambavanthaudu is born during the Prayalam and in between Srusti time his age is still a mystery for now. No one knows the date when he was born.

When Shri Maha Vishnu was born and when he was in Threta Yugam his life is 6 Manvantara (306, 72 million years). According to Kamba Ramayana every Chathur Yugam. Shri Maha Vishnu will be born every Chathur Yugam. Jambavantha say that he has seen every avatar of Shri Maha Vishnu.

We can say Jambavantha was born way before the Rama Avatar. In Valmiki Ramayana there are two References one is In Kishi Kenda Kanda to reach Lanka they need a warrior who can jump more 100 Jonas Vanara Sainam.

When Angadu ask who can jump how many Jonas, then Vanara sena warriors will say from 10 to 80 Jonas. When it is Jambavanthaudu turn he will say he can only jump 90 Jonas as he is in his old age.

When he was young, Vishnu Trivikram Rupam I have crossed the Bhoomi 21 times. Trivikram Rupam means when Vishnu came in Vamana Rupam he extended to height where Bhoomi was occupied under one feet, sky (space) in other feet.

Second incident is Pala Samudram chilakdaniki they need herbs Devatha has told me I went used all my strength and bring them to the Devatha.

These are details of Jambavantha in Krueta Yugam. Moving to Treta Yugam.

Sugriva ministers are Hanuman, Neela, Suhotra, Sarare, Saragulma, Gaja, Gavaaksha, Gavaaya, Susena, Rushba, Minada, Viveda Vijaya, Gandamadana, Ulka Muka, Asanga last one Vali Putra Angadu.

Hanuman forgets about his strength and power then Jambavanthudu will help Hanuman to know his power. In Ramayana Kishi kanda when kishi Kanda is about end Jambavnthudu calls Hanuman and say everything about his life then Hanuman knows his strength go search for Seetha.

Shri ram send Hanuman for multiverse & space

When time is coming for shri ram to leave the world go to Vaikuntam he know that Hanuman will not allow and he even fights the Yama Dharma Raja.

the universe is vast there are many worlds and multiverse he simple teaches hanuman that matter can not destroyed or created it is just transferred to another place he starts his leela.

For that he think of a plan and he throws his ring in a small hole in the earth he throws the ring into it and ask the Hanuman to bring the ring of Shri Ram.

His plan is send Hanuman in form Sukashma rupam. then hanuman takes the form of small size which is Sukashma Rupam he starts his journey.

The hole is very deep and he cannot see the outside world after going into the vast and deep at a point he sees the land there according to our Puranas the sarpa lokam snake Vasuki was seen.

The king of the sarpa lokam Vasuki he greets the Vasuki and says that Shri Ram lost his ring I came to search for his ring.

Then Vasuki ask which Shri Ram ring you came then Hanuman got confused while he was about to say Vasuki show a place.

Hanuman goes to that place and he sees many gold rings and takes the ring in his hand see that it is Bhagavan Shri Ram. He know that this ring belong to Shri ram and about to starts his journey his happiness flourishes in few seconds when he looks at the other side he sees same ring like that when he look in detail of the mountain it was not mountain but ring of Shri Ram hanuman on seeing this dint even utter a word he was shocked and surprised on seeing this.

He asks Vasuki help then he replies like this your devotee of shri ram if you dint know who know it. This explains that there many universe and multiverse in this world.

This shows us how advance our tradition and far more advance then the science which we live.

Endless cycle of creation and destruction is there in this universe.

WE have remembered the story while some advance country take this words based on the books started the science research based on our culture and tradition. **This is called stimulation hypothesis theory.**

Chapter 8

Brothers of Hanuman

They were very strong, but were present in Brahmanda Purana, They all were born through union of Mata Anjaniji and Kesariji. Hanumanji was eldest and strongest among them and he is the only Brahmachari among them.

Kesari married the daughter of Kunjara named Anjana. That lady of great purity and good fortune went to a park named Puṃsavana. Vāyu (the wind-god) made advances to the lady who was proud of her youth.

Hanumān was born of her by her union with Vayu the (source of) life into the entire universe.

The sons of Kesari were well known here as well as in the heaven. The eldest among them all was Hanuman. Matiman is remembered as the son after him.

Others were Srutiman, Ketuman and the intelligent Dhṛtimān. All the brothers of Hanumān were well established along with suitable and befitting wives. The sons were thus established by their father. They were blessed with sons and grandsons. Hanumān was a Brahmacārin (observer of the vow of celibacy). He was not joined in wedlock with any woman. He was like another Garuḍa in speed and extensive expedition.

Neela the great warrior Vanarasena

Rama sethu was build by Neeludu. He is the commander-in-chief of the Varanasena army under the Vanara king Sugriva, and described as leading the army in Rama battle aginst the rakshasa as king Ravana of Lanka.

Neela is son of Agnideva (God of fire) and as Kapishreshtha. Sugriva order Neela to assemble the Vanaras. So that they can be sent to locate sita. The Neela as a member of the search party that headed in the southern direction in search of Seetha mata.

The Ramayana credits Nala as the sole builder of the Rama setu bridge across the ocean between Rameswara and Lanka, enabling force of Rama to pass over to Lanka. However the Ramacharitamanasa credit Nala and his brother Neela for the bridge creation.

Neela heads the vanara army in the battle led by Rama against Ravana and his rakshasa army. The Ramayana tells of Neela facing the rakshasa Nikumbha. Though injured by the rakshasa, Neela picks up the chariot wheel of Nikumbha and kills him with it.

Neela also fights a fierce battle with Prahasta. The rakshasa shoots many arrows at Neela who, unable to escape, bears them calmly with closed eyes.

Later, when Prahasta dashes towards Neela with a mallet, the vanara fights back with rocks and finally hurls a huge boulder at him, thus slaying him. Neela also battles with Ravana, jumping onto his chariot.

Neela and Hanuman together battle with the rakshasas Trishira and Mahodara, when Neela kills Mahodara with a rock. The Mahabharata states that he slays the rakshasa

Pramathi in the battle. The Kamba Ramayana portrays him as being defeated and struck unconscious by Meghanada, Ravana's son.

Nala the great warrior Vanarasena

Nala , is the son of Vishwakarma , who is credited as the engineer of the Rama Setu, a bridge across the ocean between Rameswaram and Lanka, identified with modern-day Sri Lanka, so forces of the god Rama can pass over to Lanka. The bridge is also known as Nala Setu, the bridge of Nala.

Along with Nala, another vanara who his twin brother is called Neela is also credited as the builder of the bridge. Nala is described as the architect of the vanaras. He is described as the son of the architect god Vishwakarma. Nala is also described to have fought in the battle between Rama and Ravana, the king of Lanka.

Rama, aided by an army of vanaras (monkeys), reached the end of land and wanted to cross over to Lanka. Rama worships the god of the ocean, Varuna and requests him to make way. When Varuna does not appear before Rama, Rama starts shooting various weapons at the sea, which starts drying up. A terrified Varuna pleads to Rama.

Though he refuses to give way, he gives Rama a solution. He tells Rama that Nala, the son of Vishwakarma - the architect of the gods, is amongst his vanara army; Nala has the necessary expertise of an architect, owing to a boon from his divine father. Varuna suggests that Rama construct a bridge across the ocean to Lanka, under the supervision of Nala.

Nala volunteers for the task and also comments that the arrogance of the Ocean (Varuna) was tamed by Rama with a threat when love had failed. The vanaras fell mighty trees, and collect logs of wood and giant boulders and cast them in the sea. With the help of the vanara army, Nala completes the 30 miles (48 km) (ten yojana) bridge in just five days. Rama and his army pass over it and reach Lanka, where they prepare to fight Ravana Rama, aided by an army of vanaras (monkeys), reached the end of land and wanted to cross over to Lanka.

Rama worships the god of the ocean, Varuna and requests him to make way. When Varuna does not appear before Rama, Rama starts shooting various weapons at the sea, which starts drying up. A terrified Varuna pleads to Rama. Though he refuses to give way, he gives Rama a solution. He tells Rama that Nala, the son of Vishwakarma - the architect of the gods, is amongst his vanara army; Nala has the necessary expertise of an architect, owing to a boon from his divine father.

Varuna suggests that Rama construct a bridge across the ocean to Lanka, under the supervision of Nala. Nala volunteers for the task and also comments that the arrogance of the Ocean (Varuna) was tamed by Rama with a threat when love had failed. The vanaras fell mighty trees, and collect logs of wood and giant boulders and cast them in the sea. With the help of the vanara army, Nala completes the 30 miles (48 km) (ten yojana) bridge in just five days. Rama and his army pass over it and reach Lanka, where they prepare to fight Ravana

The Kamba Ramayana portrays Nala also in charge of creating living quarters for the army of Rama in Lanka. He creates a city of tents of gold and gems for the army; but builds a simple house of bamboo and wood and grass beds for himself.

Nala fights in the battle led by Rama against Ravana and his rakshasa army. Nala is described to be seriously wounded by the arrows shot by Ravana's son Indrajit. Nala kills a rakshasa called Tapana in battle. The Mahabharata describes him fighting a giant called Tundaka.

Angada the great warrior Vanarasena

Angada is a son of the powerful vanara king Vali, and his wife Tara. He is the nephew of Sugriva. After Rama and Sugriva kill his father, Angada joins Rama's forces to rescue Sita from Ravana's captivity.

Angada and Tara are instrumental in reconciling Rama and his brother, Lakshmana, with Sugriva, after the king fails to fulfill his promise to help Rama find and rescue his wife. Together, they are able to convince Sugriva to honour his pledge to Rama, instead of spending his time carousing and drinking.

Sugriva then arranges for vanaras to help Rama and organises the monkey army that will battle Ravana's demonic host. Angada leads the particular search party, which consists of Hanuman and Jambavanta and is able to find Sita, Rama's wife.

A legend goes by that no one could move Angada's leg. Just before the war, Rama sends Angada to Ravana's court as a peace messenger to give him one last chance to send Sita back to him and stop the war. Angada travels to Ravana's court, and issues him a last warning but Ravana retorts by stating that his father, Vali, is his friend.

Angada, however, rejects Ravana's stance, and retorts by saying that there was nothing as divine as serving Rama, and then proceeds to mock Ravana for his foolishness and pride, in front of the entire court. He challenges the present courtiers to move his leg, upon which he promises that he would retreat from the island, forgetting about rescuing Sita.

Almost all courtiers take turns to move his leg, but fail to even give it a budge. Even Indrajita, the most powerful son of Ravana, is unable to move the leg. Seeing Indrajita defeated, Ravana rises in fury, and proceeds to accept the challenge, upon which Angada moves his leg out of the way, and Ravana's crown falls off. When the king reaches for his crown, Angada rhetorically wonders why Ravana wishes to touch his leg, and that touching the feet of Rama would be much more fruitful instead.

He hurls the crown with such force that it is supposed to have landed at Rama's feet. The prince flies away before Ravana could seize him. Rama is pleased by this act of Angada.

In the Battle of Lanka that ensues, Angada slays many great warriors from Lanka, including, Ravana's son Narantaka, and the chief general of Ravana's army, Mahaparshva.

Angada marries the eldest daughter of the vanara Mainda, and has a son, Dhruva.

When his uncle Sugriva decides to retire from the earth and return to his father, Surya, he crowns Angada as the next king of Kishkindha, and of the vanaras.

Sarama

In the Hindu epic Ramayana, Sarama is the wife of Vibhishana, the brother of Ravana, the demon (rakshasa) king of Lanka. Sometimes, she is described as a rakshasi (demoness), at other times, she is said to have gandharva (celestial dancers) lineage.

All accounts agree that Sarama was friendly to Sita, the consort of Rama (the prince of Ayodhya and an avatar of the god Vishnu), who was kidnapped by Ravana and imprisoned in Lanka. Like her husband who sides with Rama in the war against Ravana, Sarama is kind to Sita and aids Rama. Sarama and Vibhishana had a daughter called Trijata.

Sarama does not appear in the original Ramayana. However, later interpolations – present in all recensions – added to the text of Valmiki mention her. She first appears in the episode of Maya-shirsa, the illusory head of Rama.

Ravana has abducted Sita, the wife of Rama, the prince of Ayodhya and repeatedly urges her to marry him, however Sita flatly refuses each time. After Rama with his vanara army lands on Lanka, Ravana asks his magician Vidyujihva to create an illusory severed head of Rama and his bow to convince Sita of Rama's death.

The magician complies and presents the head and bow to Sita in the Ashoka Vatika, where she is imprisoned. Sita laments in presence of Ravana seeing the head of her "dead" husband. Soon, Ravana leaves for a meeting with his ministers and the head and the bow disappear after his departure.

Sarama comes close to Sita and exposes Ravana's trickery to Sita. She says that she secretly witnessed the trick of Ravana and the head was just a product of magic. She also informs Sita that Rama has arrived in Lanka with his army headed by Sugriva and she has seen Rama with her own eyes.

She asks Sita if she can pass on any message to Rama on Sita's behalf. Sita instead requests Sarama to probe the plans Ravana had for her. Sarama finds out and informs Sita that despite the advice of his mother and wise aged ministers, Ravana refused to hand over Sita to Rama. Sarama is described as "lovely companion" and friend of Sita.

The Northern recension adds another episode about Sarama. A canto called Sarama-vakyam ("conversation with Sarama") narrates how Sarama informs Sita about the burning of Lanka by Hanuman. This episode appears before Rama comes to Lanka, when he had sent Hanuman to locate where the kidnapped Sita is.

Chapter 9

Ramayana all over world

- Ramayana in Thailand is called – Ramakien.
- Ramayana in Burma – Yamayana.
- Ramayana in Cambodia- Ramakerti.
- Ramayana in Malaysia – Hikayat.
- Ramayana in Indonesia - Kakawin Ramayana .
- Ramayana in Japan- Hobutsushu & Sambo – Ekotoba.
- Ramayana in Philippines – Maharadia Lawana.
- Ramayana in China –Liudu Ji Jing.
- Ramayana in Laos – Phra Lak Phra Ram.
- Ramayana in Russia & Mangolia – Kalmyk.
- Ramayana in Myanmar – yama Jatdaw.

The Far spread of Ramayana from Middle East Asia to south- East Asia.

Some famous Shri Ram Temples in India

- ❖ Ayodhya Ram Mandir, Uttar Pradesh.
- ❖ Triprayar Sri Rama Temple, Kerala.

* Kalaram Mandir, Nashik.
* Sita Ramachandraswamy Temple, Telangana.
* Ram Raja Temple, Madhya Pradesh.
* Kanak Bhavan Temple, Ayodhya.
* Shri Ram Tirth Temple, Amritsar.
* Kondanda Ramaswami Temple, Chikmagalur.
* Ramaswamy Temple, Tamil Nadu.
* Raghunath Temple, Jammu.

SRI KODANDA RAMASWAMY TEMPLE – Vontimitta (Ekasila Nagaram) – Andhra Pradesh (Second Ayodhya)

Kodandarama Temple

Kodandarama Temple is a Hindu temple dedicated to the god Rama, located in Vontimitta town in Vontimitta Mandalam of Kadapa District in the Indian state of Andhra. The temple, an example of Vijayanagara architectural style, is dated to the 16th century. It is stated to be the largest temple in the region.

As we know about the Valmiki the thieve who became Rama Bhakta and wrote epic Ramayana. In the same way the Vontimitta Ramalayam was built by two thieves named Vontadu and Mittadu.

Who got a change of attitude after having Darshana of Lord Srirama. Thus this place got the name Vontimitta. Previously the village was called Ekasilanagaram. These brothers after cultivating paddy in their 2 acres of land each, kept the grains in two separate heaps.

The elder brother Vontadu asked his brother to go for lunch. After his brother Mittadu went for lunch, Vontadu thought that my brother is innocent, how will he sustain his family. Thinking he took 10 bags baskets of full heap of grains from his share mixed it with his brothers share. After that his brother came and asked him to go to for lunch.

As his brother left Mittadu thought that my brother with his large family of four girls, mother, and grandmother may be having difficult in running the family. Thinking he took 20 baskets of heap mixed with his brothers hare.

The brothers got such good generous and good virtues after the divine Darshana of Lord Sri Rama. They left robbery and built the Kodanda Ramalya.

Another story:

This story of Imambeg-Imambeg served under Abdul Nadi Khan who ruled cuddapah in 1640 A.D. While on the way to Siddavattam fort, because of scorching heat, he stopped to get water for his horses. While resting on the

Verandan of the temple, he saw the people there debating about the existence of god.

The Nawab wanted to test the supremacy of god when the doors of the temple were closed. He asked the people whether their lord would reply if called, to which the devotees said that lord would definitely reply if one calls him with whole hearted devotion.

Then Imambeg went alone near the door first prayed in urdu then called "O" Rama , "O RaghuRama", Ekasila Magadarama, 3 times. Then on third time he heard saying "O". The Nawab was over whelmed. He happily prostrated before the Lord and had darshana of Rama. He well constructed the northeast side of the temple.

Muslims worship the lord and pray for the fulfilment of their wishesh.

Message from Ramayana

- **Power of Bad Association:** It was a known fact in Ayodhya that Kaikeyi loved Lord Rama more than his own son Bharath, then how could she become so evil. It is by her bad association with Mantara.

- **Attachment to service & not to the position:** Lord Ram was willing to become the king as a service to Maharaj Dasarath and He was also willing to go to the forest as a service to His father.

- **Mission of Life should be to vanquish the demoniac tendencies in our heart:** Lord Ram's purpose to kill the demons was fulfilled by His banishment to the forest.

- **Even extreme reversals if taken in the proper spirit will help us fulfill our mission in life:** For example, Law of gravity is only in effect in the Earth's sphere and not beyond. So also Laws of material nature act only in material consciousness not in spiritual consciousness.

- **Ram or Aaram, A test for every seeker:** Citizens of Ayodhya wanted to go with Lord Ram to forest and leave behind all the comforts (Aaram) of the City Ayodhya.

- **Alertness in Spiritual Life:** Lord Ram leaves Ayodhyavasis when they were asleep. If one is inattentive or lazy, one will loose taste in Bhakti.

- **(Sometimes) Saintly persons might cause pain to others not to hurt them but benefit them:** Bharat disowns Kaikeyi, or Prahlad disregards Hiranyakashipu, a Doctor may cause pain (operation) to patient to cure him.

- **Goal is to please the Lord:** For Bharat, he wanted to stay in the forest which was easier than to return and rule the Kingdom but he did it to please Lord Ram.

- **Lord is the Proprietor:** Bhoktaram Yajna tapasam (Bhagavad Gita 5.29). Bharat was ruling the kingdom on Lord Ram's behalf by keeping the Paduka's on the Throne. We are only caretakers, He is the real proprietor, He can give and take away. The Caretaker acts according to the will of the owner.

- **Anybody can make a show of greatness:** The reversals test us who we are. When Lakshmana cuts Surpanaka's nose, gone was the charming form, gone was the facade and then the real ugly form manifested. One's greatness is tested by one's ability to tolerate provoking situations.

- **Bhakti (Sita) cannot be achieved by Deception:** Ravana wanted to kidnap Sitadevi by deception, but he gets Maya-Sita at the end. Greed and lust are never satiated, they lead to arrogance and envy.

- **Attachments can creates traps and make us suffer:** Marichi takes up a golden dear form to which Sitadevi developed deep attachment to have it and thus trapped Sitadevi. We should see the substance through the eyes of the scripture. Marichi was all about false promises. For example, spider web is most attractive to the fly but actually it's a trap.

- **Maya knows our weaknesses:** She can make our strength into weaknesses and take us away from the circle of instructions of great souls. Ravana uses Sitadevi's attitude to serve great souls to disobey Lakshmana.

- **Always stand by the Right:** Jatayu's integrity. Real success is to please the Lord. Jatayu lost his life fighting for Lord Ram but achieved the purpose of

Life to please the Lord. It is better to lose & win than to win & lose.

- **Patience, Determination & Enthusiasm:** Example of Shabari. Long time ago, Guru had asked her to wait for Lord Ram while all other disciples and Guru himself went back to Godhead. She showed her enthusiasm by working hard everyday to clean the place, plucking flowers & fruits for the Lord. She had complete faith in the words of Guru and patiently waited with determination. The Lord reveals only when He wants.

- **Honesty, We can't put a facade before the Lord:** Hanumanji disguises when he went to meet Lord Ram. Lord knows within who we are, we have to be honest to receive the mercy of the Lord. Lord Ram didn't speak to Hanuman for four months.

- **Obstacles on the path of Bhakti:** The demons who came to stop Hanuman during his jumping across the ocean. Mainaka (Gold Mountain) - temptation to seek comfort before achieving our real purpose. Simhika (Shadow catching demoness) - While striving for Bhakti, people will chastise, criticize and misunderstand us, we should have the willingness to tolerate. Surasa (Serpent): Being envious of people in higher position and try to stop their progress. This is jealousy of the mind. By devotional service, we have to devour Simhika who represents Envy.

- **Arrogance cannot understand wellwishers:** The world is a mirror of our own consciousness. Ravana was thinking Mandodari was envious of Sita, but actually he was envious of Lord Ram. Ravana was thinking Vibhisana was disloyal and taking the side of Lord Ram, but he was disloyal to Kubera, his cousin brother. When we think we know, we are not willing to listen to good counsel. Spiritual progress means simplicity and humility. If they are lacking, we won't listen thinking that we know better, that was Ravana.

- **Big or Small, we can swim the ocean of Samsara by chanting Lord Ram's holy name:** Big or Small, all the stones floated by writing Lord Ram's name.

- **Pride or Attachment leads to loss of intelligence:** dhyayato visayan pumsah (Bhagavad Gita 2.62). Every stage of this sloka was exhibited by Ravana. Loss of intelligence - Even when all his stalwart warriors including Kumbakarna, Indrajit died but he still didn't give up.

- **Hearing about the Lord - Revival of dormant love:** Lord Ram being Paramatma in the heart of everyone including Ravana could have killed him just by turning off Ravana's heart. But the Lord and His pleasure potency Sitadevi went through this whole ordeal so that we can hear about the Lord and revive our dormant love.

- **Righteousness:** Vibhishana comes to take shelter of Lord Ram, all the monkeys were against, except Hanumanji. Vibhishana was willing to be misunderstood or even chastised to surrender to the Lord.

- **Counsel and Advise in battle against Illusion:** In battle against Illusion, at every stage association of devotees to put us straight without which we will fall. Lord Ram doesn't need but takes the counsel of Vibhishana.

- **Grace of a Sadhu needed to kill demons within:** Agastya muni had given a divine arrow to Lord Ram.

That arrow was used by Lord Ram to kill Ravan by piercing his heart.

- **Welcoming the Lord in hearts with lamps:** That is Dipavali festival. Lord Ram is welcomed back into Ayodhya with lamps. Dipavali is not just physical fire but lighting the hearts with light of Lord's grace and process of devotional service. When heart is fully illuminated, then we can experience Lord Ram within ourself. When our love awakens, in that love, compassion for all living beings awakens. Then Ramrajya is awakened within the heart and then without (i.e. out in the world).

About the Author

T. Krishna Dinesh is a Management Graduate who specialises in human   relations. Being brought up in a traditional background he developed a sense of interest in the purana gadhas told by his grandparents. This is an attempt to rekindle the stories all alike for those whether they had the privilege or not in their childhood.

please write to booklove788@gmail.com to

www.ingramcontent.com/pod-product-compliance
Lightning Source LLC
Chambersburg PA
CBHW051455140726
47987CB00006B/2730